CW01085992

At the Bay

At the Bay

Klavs Skovsholm

PARTRIDGE
A Penguin Random House Company

To order additional copies of this book, contact
Toll Free 0800 990 914 (South Africa)
+44 20 3014 3997 (outside South Africa)
orders.africa@partridgepublishing.com

www.partridgepublishing.com/africa

Other Books by Klavs Skovsholm

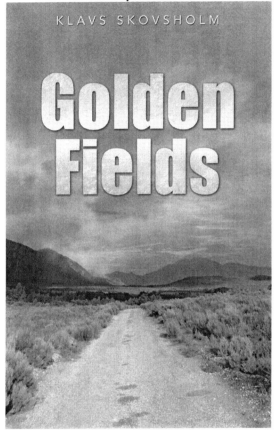

"Golden Fields is a story of adventure, love and war. The setting takes you from Southern Africa to Flanders in the period between the Boer War and WWI. The historical event which unfold are seen through the eyes of elderly lesbian couple, Theodora Villiers and Lily Wood, and of their loved ones."

To my mother
For coaching blind rowers in her youth

History is a wonderful canvas upon which to draw a story. *But be warned*: artistic license implies that *At the Bay* cannot be counted on for historical accuracy.

Although the story in 'At the Bay' is intertwined with my first book *Golden Fields*, it can be read independently.

Acknowledgements

Special thanks go to Simon's Town Historical Society and Simon's Town Museum for their help in getting many details right. I sincerely hope that they indulge me when it comes to my artistic license with history relating to their beautiful little town.

Heart-felt thanks also go to my friends Colin Robertson and Triene-Mie Le Compte, both fellow writers, for their great input and lovely ideas. It is due to their insistence, as well as that of many others, to be able to spend more time with Theodora Villiers and Lily Wood, that I set out to write *At the Bay*.

South Africa facts sheet

1652	Dutch East India Company establishes shipping station at the Cape
1795	Dutch lose the Cape to the British
1803	Dutch resume control
1806	Second British occupation of the Cape begins
1815	British rule at the Cape confirmed after the suppression of a rebellion by Afrikaans-speaking settlers
1820	4 000 British settlers arrive in the Cape
1834	Slavery abolished in the Cape following a decision by the British Parliament
1835	The Great Trek. Many Afrikaans-speaking farmers (Boers) leave the Cape Colony moving north of the Orange River where they establish independent republics, but the majority of Afrikaners remain in the Cape
1838	Following successful fights against the Zulus, many Afrikaners begin to settle in the Natal
1843	The British annex the Natal as a colony
1852	Sand River Convention confirms independence of the Transvaal Republic
1854	Bloemfontein Convention confirms independence of the Orange Free State

1870	Diamond rush to Kimberley which is subsequently annexed to the Cape Colony
1877	The British proclaim Transvaal a British colony
1880-1	Transvaal President Kruger rebels against the British rule: First Boer War
1881	Pretoria Convention: Transvaal Republic obtains limited independence
1884	London Convention: Transvaal Republic obtains greater independence
1886	Gold rush to Witwatersrand (Johannesburg area) begins
1895	500-strong private police force backed by British industrialists seek unsuccessfully to occupy Witwatersrand
1896	Cape Prime Minister, Cecil John Rhodes, resigns because of his implication in the unsuccessful occupation
1897	One of the masterminds behind the future Second Boer War, Sir Alfred Milner takes over as the British High Commissioner at the Cape
1899	September: the British decide to send 10 000 troops to defend Natal
1899	October: Kruger sends troops into the Natal in response to British demands for equal rights of its citizens in the Afrikaner republics
1899-1902:	War rages north off the Cape Colony

1901	Queen Victoria dies
1902	April: First peace negotiations in Pretoria May: final peace negotiations in Vereeniging with signature of surrender terms in Pretoria a couple of weeks later
1909	The British Parliament adopts the first constitution of The Union of South Africa

Simon's Town, South Africa, February 1900

18 year-old Peter Smith stood on the floating pier of Simon's Town rowing club, watching the calm waters. Not a wind was stirring and the sun had just started to come up. Soon its rays would be bathing the mountains, the harbour and the bay in golden light.

"What an exceptional morning," he thought.

He turned as he heard a plank in the pier creak behind him. He immediately recognized the red hair of his rowing partner, Riaan Meershoek, who was coming up the pier accompanied by his coloured houseboy, Kalim. Their progress created a rocking sensation like waves lapping against the pier.

"Morning, Riaan," Peter said as Kalim made Riaan stop in front of him. His voice immediately made Riaan direct his gentle face towards him. Riaan had always been blind and he could only sense the shadows of light and dark. Peter looked at Riaan's brown eyes which were open, but without life. He had a straight nose, and his skin was lightly golden and freckled where he had tanned. Peter, with his darker complexion and black hair, tanned a much deeper colour and withstood exposure to the sun much better.

"Good morning to you, too, Peter!" He let go of Kalim, moved forward a little and touched Peter's arms with his hands. "It's a really quiet morning, isn't it?"

Then it struck Peter that this morning would be just perfect for letting Riaan try out the new light double scull with sliding seats which the club had recently received from England.

"Riaan, I want us to row the new double scull. Are you up for it? The weather is just right."

"Of course I am. There are not that many days this calm at the Cape so we must make the best of them!"

Quickly, Peter, Riaan and Kalim got the light boat out of the boat house. Peter asked Kalim to step aside. Between Riaan and himself they would have no difficulty in carrying the boat on their own. Riaan had never helped carry a boat this light before.

Riaan ran his fingers over the polished surface of the shell. He could not decide what the shell was made of. It did not quite feel like the wood of the other boats in the club.

"What is this shell made of?" he asked in wonder.

"It's many layers of lacquered paper glued together. Waterproof, light, but fragile," Peter said with some pride as if the idea had been his own.

Gently and with great care, Peter helped Riaan into the boat after explaining to him where to put his feet.

Precision was of the essence to avoid cracks in the shell. With his sense of balance and coordination, Riaan, with a little help from Peter, found his seat with ease while he was holding on to his oars with his left hand. Kalim stood nearby with a worried expression for fear that his *baas* should fall in.

A few minutes later they were off. Riaan was in the bow seat while Peter had taken up his position in the stern seat. Tentatively at first; Riaan was not used to such a light, nimble craft under him. However, soon the boat was in balance under the two rowers. For the first time, Riaan felt the exhilarating sensation of the light boat gliding effortlessly across the calm surface. The sense of propulsion created by pushing back on his footrest took his breath away. He could also sense how the darkness was disappearing around him, increasingly feeling the warm rays of the sun on his body.

Peter, too, was thrilled with the performance of the new boat. He could feel that with the right amount of training, this double scull could be made to go very fast. Peter loved sports. In England, he had been an avid cricket player and rower. He had been reluctant to follow his family to South Africa when his father had been stationed here shortly before the outbreak of the war, but he had soon discovered that South Africa was the best playground imaginable.

Peter looked around. The golden light reflecting from the surface almost blinded him. He could not remember seeing Simon's Town look more stunning than this.

"Oh Riaan, look how beautiful!" he burst out. He stopped abruptly. His heart sank. He had not intended to remind his friend of what he could not see. He often felt pity for Riaan whom God had not allowed to see all the incredible beauty surrounding those fortunate enough to visit the Cape.

Peter need not have worried. Riaan was smiling, but all Peter could see was his red hair, the back of his rowing suit and the freckles on his shoulders. However, he stopped rowing, forcing Peter to do the same, and let the scull drift.

"Try and describe it to me, Peter, if you can… Be my eyes for a moment."

Gliding forward, holding both oars in his left hand, Peter gently placed his free hand on Riaan's back just for a moment. It felt warm and a little sweaty. Then he grabbed his oars with both hands again.

"Well… it's like a mirror. So to my eye I see the same object twice, the real object and the reflected object reproduced by the surface of the water. I see the sky reflected in the water and the mountains look as if they have identical twins descending down into the water… and the sunlight…"

"How to explain the sunlight?" he pondered.

"And the sunlight, Peter?"

"… I don't know how to describe it."

"And the sunlight is warm, right?" Riaan said with irony.

"Yes! The sunlight is warm!" Peter laughed while Riaan turned his face towards the warm sun.

"I think I love you, Riaan," Peter suddenly thought. For a moment he suppressed his urge to place his hand on Riaan's back. "But you will never see my loving glance. If you had sight, it would only be for girls." These feelings frightened him, but he could not help himself. Riaan's good looks and positive attitude had drawn him like a magnet since he had first met him not too long ago when his father had been stationed at the Naval Station.

"Riaan, will you row with me at the Table Bay Championships on 24 May?"

Peter knew he should not have asked, but his urge to be around Riaan was too strong. "In this boat?"

"Do you reckon they'd let us? This boat is so different from all the heavy wooden ones."

"Yes, I have made inquiries. Some of the other clubs, like Alfred's and Britannia, have got them already. So this year there'll be a race for these light ones too."

"That's a deal then!" Riaan answered immediately. Peter's heart leapt with joy.

"Are you ready to continue, Peter?"

"Yes."

"OK then. From backstops, half slide."

On their way back to the rowing club, they passed close by a naval ship at anchor. A sailor, wearing only khaki shorts was busy washing the deck and saw them coming. He took a small break and leaned over the railing to study the unusual sculling boat. Looking up, Peter hungrily rested his eyes on the sailor's muscular torso. As the sailor winked and grinned broadly at him, Peter blushed.

April the same year

Lily Wood was tending to the white roses planted alongside the house she shared with her Afrikaans partner, Theodora Villiers, in the small village of Straateind on the edge of the Karoo in the Western Cape. They had shared this house for some years since Theodora had become a widow. It was a simple but spacious Karoo house with high windowless gables, wooden shutters and a black thatched roof. Theodora and Lily loved their house.

Theodora and Lily had left Stellenbosch for Straateind to live a life according to their own ideas. Lily had very little family, except for a couple of cousins. Theodora had left behind her married daughter Mariette and her grandchild Antonius. Mariette was married to the local judge in Stellenbosch. Their moving to Straateind, or more specifically the fact that the two mature ladies had moved in together, had led to a fallout between Theodora and Mariette. Mariette did not approve. This caused Theodora much pain, but she chose to hide it. Besides, she was convinced that following her heart was the right thing to do.

Although it took the best part of the day to reach Stellenbosch by horse, Straateind had become much more accessible with a recently built train stop only an hour away by donkey cart. Cape Town was now easy to reach in a day.

Straateind was surrounded by mountains. Only one road led in and out. Theodora and Lily liked the village too. They did not have much contact with their neighbours. They were seen as the eccentric outsiders, especially Theodora who, despite her Afrikaner origins, was prone to dressing unconventionally and rarely attended church. On the other hand, Lily would always dress appropriately in long skirts and hid her hair under a straw hat. It had been rumored that Theodora had been seen wearing riding breeches, riding a horse like a man.

Things had been really good for them in Straateind until Britain had gone to war with the Boer republics up north in the previous month of October 1899. This had dragged the British colony in the Western Cape into war with its Northern neighbours. Most of Straateind's inhabitants were Afrikaners who, although they had lived under British rule for a long time, had little love left for the British. The daily reporting of atrocities in the war some 800 miles away meant that Lily, being English, was met with much coldness. So the couple had become outsiders even more than before.

*

When Theodora returned from *Meneer* Pretorius' general store she placed her basket on the kitchen table. Lately, only she would go to the general store. Lily refused after having been received so coldly that she had walked out feeling humiliated.

Through the window she caught sight of Lily outside her workshop in the garden behind their house. Lily was busy cleaning some paint brushes at a table. She wore an apron with a multitude of paint stains. Lily looked up as Theodora appeared in the garden. She felt a warm glow in her heart seeing her partner and interrupted her scrubbing of brushes. She wore heavy gloves to protect her delicate hands from the chemicals she used to clean them.

Theodora leaned forward and kissed Lily on her hair while Lily was careful to hold her brushes away from her for fear that she might stain Theodora's light blue dress. Then Theodora caught sight of an official-looking envelope on the table.

"So, what's this?" she asked pointing with her chin towards the envelope. "Looks like Giles the postman was here while I was gone."

Theodora was happy that Giles would occasionally call on Lily for a chat, even when he had no mail to deliver. Being Scottish, he did not shun Lily for being English like so many of their Afrikaner neighbours did. Giles also had a sweet tooth and he always appreciated the prospect of a cup of tea and a piece of one of the many cakes Theodora loved to bake. Although Lily was extremely good at immersing herself in her painting and in doing all the small jobs around the house and garden, she took immense pleasure in Giles' visits and their witty conversations. Giles was just the man for that and he always made Lily laugh. Laughs had been few and far apart since the war broke out.

"That's a letter from my Cousin Robert inviting us for the official function to celebrate the Queen's birthday next month." Cousin Robert was one of Lily's remote cousins who was the admiral at the Naval Station in Simon's Town. They received an invitation every year but had not gone since they had moved to Straateind because of the travelling involved.

"Maybe we should go this year, Lily? With the new train stop it will be so much easier to get there."

She did not say so, but Theodora was thinking that Lily could benefit from a break away from Straateind. A break in a place where she would not be shunned for being English. Lily's face lit up as if she had not considered that they would go, but she also looked a little hesitant, Theodora noticed.

"If we do go…" Lily started. "Maybe we could go for a couple of weeks. I don't want to stay with Cousin Robert all that time… maybe a few days in a nice boarding house somewhere else on the coast, like Muizenberg, and a few days at the British Hotel in Simon's Town?" Lily's face had by now regained its usual radiance which Theodora loved so well.

Theodora was delighted to see how this idea lifted Lily's spirits in a way she had not seen for quite a while. Lily had grown up on the coast close to Simon's Town, so she felt much more connected to the sea than Theodora who had always lived inland.

Had Theodora been able to read Lily's mind, she would have seen a glimpse of the False Bay beaches through the eyes of a little girl taking brisk walks on the beach, felt the wind in the hair of that little girl, and heard the cries of seagulls overhead. Lily's memories were so vivid that, for an instant, she could smell the salt in the air and, on her skin, feel the warm grains of sand carried with the wind.

"I think that's a lovely idea, my dear," Theodora said. "Do you want me to write to Cousin Robert or will you do it?

Mid-May 1900

Lily could not find words to express her joy over going to the seaside in Muizenberg. Much as she loved the arid, rugged landscapes around Straateind, the sea stirred different emotions in her all together. As the train was approaching the sea, she had noticed the change of brilliance in the light. Having rained a little that same morning, Table Mountain could be seen from even further afield than usual, towering over Cape Town in the clear sunshine.

They changed trains at the Cape Town station where they boarded the Southern Line to Muizenberg. As the train was making its way through the leafy suburbs on the southern side of Table Mountain, Lily had faint memories of her time in England at a very young age.

"Look at all those oak trees, Theo. I think the driveway to my parents' house had oak trees like these," she said gaily while she tried to recall clearly her faint memories.

"Even so they are out of place," Theodora thought. She had always held the view that with the immense variety of plants in the Cape there was no point in importing any plants from abroad. She briefly pondered the fact that the many enormous oak trees along the track owed their survival to their growing too fast in South Africa to provide suitable timber for building boats, which was the reason that they had been planted in the first place.

"What else do you remember from your English childhood, my dear?" Theodora asked so as not to spoil Lily's pleasure at seeing the trees.

"Oh, very little," Lily laughed. "But you know that, I was an only child of four and half when I arrived here. My childhood really only started that morning when we sailed into Cape Town and I saw Table Mountain for the first time."

"My first vivid childhood memory is of me sitting on my grandmother's lap eating *Melk tart* under a tree. I must have been about three," Theodora said happily.

*

On one of their morning strolls in Muizenberg over the coming days, Lily and Theodora admired the many large houses which had been built along the coast. About a decade earlier, the railway line had made the small communities along False Bay easily accessible.

At one point they stopped in front of a small cottage a little south of the station: a small almost featureless cottage with a corrugated iron roof.

"I've heard that this little cottage belongs to our former prime minister Cecil Rhodes," Lily said.

"Really? Who would have thought that? Look at the other houses around. I wonder why one of the richest men in the country would be satisfied with such a small hut?" Theodora said.

"You know, Theo, he does own the Groote Schuur Estate, so he's not exactly short of space, is he?"

"No, I suppose he isn't," Theodore chuckled.

"Maybe he has one thing in common with the two of us: he also wants to live a simple life? You also left your impressive Cape Dutch house in Stellenbosch, remember? To live simply in Straateind," Lily said with a smile in her voice. "And look at the views from this place!" she continued.

The cottage stood at the nape of the Cape Peninsula, on the coastline which sweeps round to Simon's Town and on to the Cape of the Good Hope. From where Lily and Theodora were standing, they could see the broad aspect of the beginning of the Indian Ocean and immediately behind, the Muizenberg Mountains were rising.

"No palatial home has any view better than this," Theodora thought. Suddenly, she felt a little pang of home sickness as she thought of the view of the mountains and the clear blue skies in Straateind from her favorite bench in front of their house.

*

Theodora watched Lily descending the stairs down to the beach from the promenade in Muizenberg. Lily was wearing a light white summer dress and a large straw hat. The material of Lily's dress was fluttering in the wind, but the hairpins kept her brimmed hat firmly in place. Lily carried her drawing materials under one arm and held a small stool in her hand as she set out to find a suitable spot on the beach.

"This light and the vibrant colours call for a totally different choice of paints than at home," Lily thought." I must try and capture this bright light on the surface of the sea" The light on the sea reminded her of some lovely prints of works of Scandinavian painters depicting life at the seaside which she had recently seen. She had found the prints so inspiring that she now wanted to have a go at painting in the same impressionist style. So she planned to do sketches on the beach which she could later finish in oils back in Straateind.

From the promenade Theodora waved at Lily on the beach, but Lily was so absorbed in her own thoughts that she did not notice. Theodora kept watching her partner striding across the white sand, a smile playing on her lips.

"At a distance, she could be mistaken for a much younger person with her slender figure," Theodora mused. "Especially in that dress when she moves so energetically." Theodora's memories transported her back to a time when she had first laid eyes on Lily Wood. "You are as adorable as you have ever been, my English Lily. I am so glad that we treated ourselves to this little break," she thought.

Then she turned her back away from Lily on the beach and left the promenade making for the main street which had shops and pavements on either side of the road. Theodora had made a list of items she would look for while in Muizenberg because choice was very limited in Straateind.

As Theodora was proceeding up the main street, her eye caught sight of a tall, slim young man with red hair walking towards her. She noticed the redhead's beautiful face with a straight nose and fine features. She then realized that he was blind because he was walking with another man, a Coloured, who led him by the arm. They were about the same age. The coloured man was a fair bit shorter than the red haired man. They were calmly walking towards the spot where Theodora had stopped. She noticed how people made room for them, some while eyeing the coloured man.

Theodora was surprised. It had just dawned on her that she knew who this young redhead was. Compared to a mere boy when she had last seen him, he had now grown into a young man. He was Riaan Meershoek, son of the local doctor in Simon's Town.

So she walked right up to the approaching men and stopped in front of Riaan who stopped, too, sensing someone in front of him. Now the coloured man looked uneasy.

"Yes?" Riaan said and straightened up in the face of this person whom he could not see. It would not have been the first time that someone would take objection to him being accompanied by a coloured man on the pavement.

"Riaan Meershoek?" Theodora said. She sent the coloured man a small comforting smile and gave him a nod of her head in recognition of his being there.

"That's correct," Riaan replied with some reserve.

"You may not remember me. I'm Theodora Villiers. You met me and my friend Lily Wood some years ago when we paid a visit to your father."

Theodora could see on Riaan's face that his mind was still blank as to who she was. So she tried again.

"You may remember that I read you the story *Rikki-Tikki-Tavi*? That was some years ago. I had come to visit your father and mother and I read for you at bedtime."

"Yes! I remember that!" he burst out and reached out for Theodora. Theodora grabbed his hand to avoid any further embarrassment. Kalim let go of Riaan's arm and stepped to the edge of the pavement where he took up position looking down at his feet. Theodora noticed this sign of respect which she felt was exaggerated, but he was not her servant, she reasoned.

Theodora also remembered Riaan's mother later questioning her choice of children's stories. The tale of the evil cobras had caused Riaan to have nightmares for several nights in a row.

Theodora took a closer look at Riaan. He had turned into a very handsome young man.

"Will you read for me again, Miss Villiers?" Riaan asked.

"Would you like me to?"

"I would like that very much, Miss Villiers. Not that there is anything wrong with good old Kalim's voice, but a female voice would make a welcome change."

He now smiled and reached out in the empty air to pat Kalim on the shoulder so as to include him. Kalim grabbed Riaan's hand to reassure him of his whereabouts, and Riaan gave Kalim's hand a good squeeze.

"*Baie dankie Baas,*" Kalim mumbled and started to relax.

"Riaan, please call me Miss Theodora."

"Miss Theodora," he repeated.

"Would you care to sit and talk for a moment, Riaan? There's a bench here in the shade in front of the shops." She started to feel tired and hot after all the exposure to the sun and wind that morning.

Riaan nodded.

So Theodora directed him away from Kalim to the bench where they sat down.

"So what brings you to Muizenberg, Riaan?" Theodora asked.

"I wanted to buy a book. The choice is limited in Simon's town. All the sailors at the Naval Station are more interested in lighter entertainment. My parents give me a small allowance, so I'm able to save a little money and buy a book from time to time. Thanks to Kalim I can read as many books as I can get my hands on. Braille books are expensive and hard to come by, so I've only got a few. Kalim and I came down on third class so as not to waste money," he said with a chuckle.

Theodora glanced at Kalim, who now stood respectfully with his back turned to them. "I have a feeling Kalim is a nice person," she thought.

"So you really like to read?" Theodora asked.

"Oh yes, Miss Theodora. I love to read. I'd love to go to university like my older brothers. But father thinks it's impossible... with the war and ... everything." He pointed briefly at his blind eyes.

"How wonderful that you, Kalim, can read for Riaan," Theodora said raising her voice to address the coloured boy. "Do you also like to read, Kalim?"

Kalim turned around with a surprised air at being addressed like this.

"*Ja, mevrouw*, I like reading too," he said and grinned.

"What would you like to study, Riaan?"

"I like English and literature. Maybe Arabic..."

"Arabic?"

"I cannot imagine that would be something his parents would want him to study," she thought and was about to comment on it, but restrained herself. "Never mind what he wants to study, as long as he is passionate about it," she thought, reconciling herself with Riaan's unusual idea, recalling how she had always encouraged her grandchild Antonius to explore ideas freely.

"Yes, you see… can I confide in you, Miss Theodora?" Riaan asked as he turned his head towards Kalim. They both looked uneasy because of the question.

"But of course, you may. What we talk about will stay between you and me," Theodora said while looking at Kalim to reassure him of her good intentions.

Riaan leaned forward. "I have begun to learn about the Koran," he said in a low voice.

"Really? How do you manage that?" She looked questioningly at both of them.

"Kalim's a Muslim and one day I asked him some questions about his religion. So he took me to see his uncle, the local imam in Simon's Town. There is a small mosque a few streets away from my father's house up the hill. With so many Muslims in town I thought I should know a bit more about them."

"Very admirable, Riaan. Not many men your age would show the same degree of consideration."

"Or many people around here, for that matter," she thought.

"Thank you, Miss Theodora. But I think it's just my nature to be curious about all the things I cannot see." He fell quiet for a moment.

"So now we go every week and spend some time with the imam. The Koran is really very interesting," he continued enthusiastically. "And I like the sound of Arabic, too."

Theodora had heard Arabic spoken on a few occasions, but she had not found the sound of it very appealing.

"Remember this, Riaan," she said warmly. "The eyes are useless if the mind is blind." Then she squeezed his hand.

"Thank you, Miss Theodora. I shall always remember that."

"And rest assured, both of you, that your secret is safe with me. We wouldn´t want any trouble, would we?"

Still Theodora was worried for Riaan and Kalim, knowing how deeply religious many Christians were in the Cape, especially respectable Afrikaner families such as Riaan's.

A moment of silence passed between them while Riaan and Kalim seemed to ponder the warning behind her reassurance.

"So except for reading, what do you do in your free time, Riaan?" she asked.

"Rowing! I love it! I am going to row in the Table Bay Championships on the Queen's Birthday next week with my rowing partner Peter Smith," he replied. "I'd love to invite you! Would you come?"

"Of course, I'll come to see you. Can I bring my best friend Lily? We'll come to Simon's Town tomorrow and stay a few days at the Admiralty." Riaan nodded his head enthusiastically in consent.

"How's Simon's Town these days?"

Riaan suddenly looked pensive.

"You may find that Simon's town has changed. There's so much activity with all the troops arriving before going to war up north and the Boer prisoners of war being shipped off to St. Helena. They have set up a big tented camp south of town for the thousands of prisoners already taken."

"They ship Boers off to St. Helena?"

"Yes, they do. There are also a lot of sick prisoners. Really a lot."

"How do you know all that?"

"My father has gone to help the navy doctor on a few occasions. The lucky ones are the ones that get shipped off."

"But that's horrific!" Theodora burst out. "Something should be done to prevent that!"

She felt her heart sink at the thought of her kinsmen being deported. Normally, she would have remained silent on the subject of the war with so many British people around. An expression of sympathy with the Boers up north would only spark strong reactions and she would risk severe punishment for helping the Boers. But among fellow Afrikaans speakers she felt more at ease.

"Indeed," Riaan said. "That's why father offered to help with the sick prisoners of war at the naval hospital."

They fell silent for a moment. Theodora was very upset, but she felt helpless. "There must be something I can do to alleviate some of this suffering," she told herself.

"I've heard that the hospital has an extraordinary volunteer who came all the way from England," Riaan continued.

"Oh really?"

"Her name is Mary Kingsley. She has been an explorer in West Africa. I came to Muizenberg to check if they had a copy of her book *Travels in West Africa*."

Lily and Theodora had read her book, so Theodora pricked up her ears at the mention of Mary Kingsley.

They had been very impressed by the accounts of these travels. Noting that neither Riaan nor Kalim were carrying any parcels, she assumed that the search for the book had been in vain.

"I've got a copy of that book back in Straateind. I shall send it to you when I get back," she promised.

"Oh, thank you, Miss Theodora," he said squeezing her hand in joy. For a brief moment Theodora caught a glimpse of the boy still inhabiting the young man's body.

*

Theodora and Lily were walking down St. George's Street to the British Hotel to meet Dr Meershoek who had sent them an invitation to join him there for tea. He stood outside the hotel waiting for them as they arrived.

"Mrs. Villiers, Miss Wood! How delightful to see you back in Simon's Town!"

"And we're delighted to be back," Lily replied.

He shook their hands while bowing slightly. It was clear to Theodora whom Riaan had his good looks from.

"Riaan did tell me that he had met the kind lady who had read *Rikki-Tikki-Tavi* to him," he continued good-humouredly.

"You didn't tell me that you had met Dr Meershoek's son," Lily said.

"Didn't I? Maybe not – anyway, I met him in Muizenberg the other day while you were making sketches on the beach," Theodora said.

"Well, shall we?" Dr Meershoek said.

"Lead the way, Doctor," Lily said gaily.

Dr Meershoek stepped forward and opened the door into the hotel. They climbed the short flight of stairs to the inner courtyard where he steered them towards a table where a slim woman got up to greet them. She was wearing a white laced-up blouse and a long black woollen skirt. Her fair hair was pinned back.

"Good evening, Miss Kingsley!" Dr Meershoek said. "May I introduce you to Mrs. Villiers and Miss Wood?"

"So here's the famous explorer," Theodora thought. "But she is so young! She looks around the age of my daughter!"

*

"Yes, as Dr Meershoek just told you, I have volunteered to nurse prisoners of war here in Simon's Town," Mary Kingsley said in her slight cockney accent which was in some contradiction to her posture. She sat upright like a real lady with both hands in her lap.

Theodora found her intriguing and could not take her eyes off her. "I cannot imagine how this impeccably dressed and softly spoken young lady marched and hacked her way through the swamps of West Africa. Even climbed Mount Cameroon!" she thought.

Theodora knew many Afrikaner women made of sterner stuff than herself, but judging from Mary Kingsley's travel accounts, she was now confronted with someone who had to be made of altogether sterner stuff than any woman she could think of. Her eyes rested so intently on Mary's pretty face that she did not notice Lily repeatedly trying to establish eye contact with her.

"Miss Kingsley is a great help to Dr Carré at the naval hospital," Dr Meershoek continued. "Most volunteers from the UK only want to nurse English soldiers. But Miss Kingsley bravely looks after the Boers – many badly wounded. And of late, more and more are dying from typhoid fever." Theodora's esteem for Mary Kingsley grew with the Doctor's last remark.

"Typhoid fever?" Lily said frightened.

"I'm afraid so," Mary said. "Many are in a really bad shape when they get here from the front."

"What are the symptoms?" Theodora asked.

She noticed that the Doctor suddenly looked ill at ease.

"More than anything," Mary said quietly. "They've got high fever and they're often suffering from a kind of muttering delirium…"

"Muttering delirium?" Lily said.

"Yes, the poor souls don't know where they are. Often they pick at things only they can see," Mary continued steadfast. "Or they get up and walk around crazily in their nightshirts."

It was clear from Dr Meershoek's expression that he did not think this conversation fit for afternoon tea among respectable ladies.

"I only understand a few words of Afrikaans," Mary continued. "So mostly their last words are lost on me, I'm afraid. I can only sit beside them and watch them die. The other day a dying young man was so bewildered that he thought I was an angel. He used the word *Engel* like in German."

"How dreadful!" Lily said. "Poor boys. They must feel so lonely in their last moments."

"However, the greatest number of them die from dehydration caused by serious diarrhoea," Mary added matter of factly, keeping her memories of the green stools, comparable to pea soup with their characteristic smell, to herself.

"Is there no cure?" Theodora asked.

"No," Dr Meershoek said. "It is, so far, the biggest killer in this war. However, I have heard that the army will soon start testing a new vaccine on the British soldiers."

Theodora could see on Lily's face that it was time to change the subject.

"Would you care for some more tea, Doctor?" she asked.

He seemed grateful for her question. Still, Theodora was resolved to see what she could do to alleviate some of the suffering. Then she caught Lily's eye and noticed that her partner was pained.

"I must admit, Miss Kingsley," Theodora said, "that I find it most admirable that you have come all the way from England to nurse Boer prisoners of war."

"Please call me Mary."

"Very well, "Theodora said a little surprised.

"I feel this war is quite unnecessary," Mary continued. "So I want to do my bit."

"Are you against Imperialism?" Lily asked.

"No, not really. I do believe that the Europeans have a role to play in Africa and that we could do a lot of good with the right people on the ground."

"Yes?" Lily said.

"Trust me. I have seen a lot of hopeless administrators in West Africa, regardless of their nationality. They were so utterly unable to even *try* and understand the local populations."

"Sounds like the average person around here," Theodora thought.

*

Like the previous times Lily had come to the Admiralty with her childhood friend Theodora, Cousin Robert put them up in separate rooms. "He always keeps up an air of respectability," Theodora mused. "It's like most people. They choose to see only what they want to see, especially when it is to their advantage to stay oblivious of reality." She walked quietly down the corridor to Lily's room to bid her goodnight, carrying a small candlestick in her hand to provide some light. She felt the carpet under her naked feet.

After a gentle knock, she opened the door and stuck her head around it, looking at Lily. She noticed in the dimmed warm light from several candles in the room that Lily had not gone to bed yet. She slipped quietly in and came towards Lily who stood with her back to Theodora. She wore a white nightgown and her long hair cascaded down over her shoulders. Lily stood quietly observing herself in the mirror. Theodora's heart swelled. Lily looked like an angel to her, one of the most beautiful women she had ever laid eyes on. As she came closer, she could see Lily's tearful eyes in the low light. Theodora stopped when she noticed. "What's wrong?" she wondered. Lily had been a little withdrawn since they had been introduced to Mary Kingsley. She quickly placed her candlestick on the dresser and came up to Lily, gently placing her hand on her shoulder and resting her head against her hair.

"My love, you are all upset?"

Lily just nodded, but said nothing.

"What's wrong?"

"Oh, look at me, Theo! I have grown into such an old women…" She started to sob quietly for fear that she would be heard in one of the other rooms. "I am not worth loving any longer…"

Lily seemed heartbroken. Theodora's mind scanned the last couple of days for events which might have caused this. "Whoever has caused my Lily this pain will have to deal with me," she thought.

"I don't think you love me any longer, Theo."

Theodora's heart skipped a beat and her gut constricted in pain over this wrong accusation.

"My darling… my Lily, but I love you and only you! Whatever has given you reason to think otherwise?" she said with conviction, fighting back her own tears. Lily was her one and only love. She turned her around and held her by the shoulders meeting her tearful gaze.

"The way you look at Mary," Lily answered painfully. "You've only had eyes for her since you met her." Silence erupted. Theodora did not believe her ears. Yes, she admitted she had been taken by Mary, who was a fair bit younger than Lily and her. In fact, Mary somehow reminded her of the younger Lily she had fallen in love with. But being in the company of Mary with all her wonderful qualities also caused a dreadful pain as it reminded her of her own daughter who was without such virtues.

Theodora took a step back and took both Lily's hands. "My love, look at you! You still have your girlish figure … your beautiful hair that I wish you would show us more often… the other day on the beach just looking at you made me dizzy, I had butterflies flutter in my stomach…" Now tears swelled up in her eyes, too. They locked eyes as they stood there, looking at each another.

Then Lily let go of Theodora's hand and she swiftly reached down and pulled her nightgown over her head. Theodora was surprised. A moment later Lily stood naked in front of her. Her milky white skin had a warm glow in the candlelight.

"Come Theo," she said, leading her to the bed. "Come lie with me like we did when we first met." Her glance was now mischievous and Theodora could not help smiling at this sudden change in Lily's mood. "But you must be quiet, Theo," Lily then giggled. "So no one hears us."

"Of course. I'll be quiet, my love. We don't want to cause Cousin Robert any embarrassment, do we?" she whispered.

*

Lily had several letters to write so Theodora decided she would go for a short walk. Since the town was under extra security she could not walk as far south as she would have liked because that was where the large tented camp for Boer prisoners had been established. She knew that several thousands of men were imprisoned there awaiting their gradual deportation to St. Helena. Dr Carré had assured her that conditions were quite satisfactory, and as part of keeping the prisoners healthy they were compelled to bathe in the sea every morning.

There was a chill in the air so she was happy that she had brought a shawl. The Cape winter was not far away, yet they were still enjoying balmy Indian summer days in the afternoons.

She looked up towards the overcrowded Palace Barracks Hospital where she knew Dr Carré, Mary and a handful of other nurses, English and Afrikaner women, set their differences aside while toiling relentlessly to look after the many wounded Afrikaners.

Mary had discreetly let her see the conditions inside the building. She had not told Lily what she had seen, because of her sensitive nature. Theodora had always considered herself to be made of solid stuff, but this experience had been truly heartbreaking. She looked around in disbelief. The walls were streaked with dirt and the paint was peeling. The place was totally crowded by the many men who had been wounded in the British artillery up north. Now, many of them had come down with typhoid fever. The stench was horrific despite the nurses' best efforts to keep the place clean and aired. The many cases of diarrhoea made the job of keeping the bedpans clean an overwhelming task.

At one point she was shocked as she came upon a tall man with long blond hair. For a moment she thought it was her own grandchild Antonius whom she thought was in the Congo working for the Belgians. She quickly walked over to the stretcher to take a closer look. Noticing that she had been mistaken, she let out a sigh of relief, which made the young man open his eyes and look at her. He held her gaze for a moment, but he did not make a sound except for his laboured breathing. She reached out and placed her hand on the burning warm moist forehead of the man. He closed his eyes again and seemed to slumber with a faint smile on his lips.

"He doesn't have far to go," Mary whispered as she gently led Theodora away from the dying man.

Theodora contemplated the painful feelings of a mother losing her son and she was embarrassed at how relieved she was realizing that the dying man was not her grandchild. But then she felt a strong pain in her stomach as her eyes slowly wandered from one dying patient to the next. Fighting back her tears, she took in the rows of narrow iron beds, squeezed together, the coarse sackcloth sheets and mud-colored blankets. She bent over and placed her hands on her stomach.

"Are you alright?" Mary asked concerned.

"I can hardly breathe," Theodora said. "All these young men were meant to grow up and have families, not to die in appalling conditions in a hospital ward where the most basic medical supplies are lacking. I would have expected the world's largest empire to be able to provide bandages, at least." She paused briefly.

"How can you deal with all this suffering, Mary?" Theodora continued as she held back her tears.

Mary looked pensive for a moment, shrugging her shoulders.

"I wasn't meant to be fragile just because I was born a women," she said. "When the suffering is too great, I look at the sun, at the positive side of life. That way the shadows are behind me," she said and smiled at Theodora who now had tears running down her cheeks.

A few days later, Theodora asked Dr Carré if she could donate some supplies to the hospital. To her dismay, he tactfully informed her that it was against the rules for a naval hospital to receive any donation from private citizens. She had left him in a state of great inner turmoil as her sense of justice had been trespassed upon. So the next day she had discreetly sent a letter to a coloured merchant in Cape Town, with whom she had traded for many years, to make inquiries as to whether he could deliver a wagon load of basic medical supplies to Simon's Town. She was still awaiting an answer.

She turned to explore the streets on the slope of the mountains above St. Georges' street. She took one of the few staircase alleys leading away from the main street. Soon she found herself in the backwaters of Simon's Town. Up here she enjoyed the beautiful view of the ocean over the roofs of the white community below, but the streets were crammed and the houses small. Mostly coloureds lived here. She mused at the differences a few hundred meters could make while studying the small poor houses.

Then she decided to seek out the small mosque Riaan had told her about. She soon found it and walked up to the door. She reached for the handle. To her surprise the door was open. She quietly opened it and peeked inside. Uncertain, she covered her hair with her shawl and stepped timidly over the threshold.

Inside, she noticed small shelves had been mounted on the wall for the congregation to put their shoes. She took her own shoes off and placed them on one of the shelves.

"What a beautiful room," she thought, admiring the emerald green carpets under her feet. The sunlight pouring through the narrow windows made the green colour sparkle.

Suddenly, she heard someone. She turned and saw a small man dressed in Western clothes but with the typical small hat worn by many Cape Muslims. He looked at her with a hard expression on her face as if he were about to tell a child off for some offence. "Or is he afraid?" she wondered.

"Mag ek U help, mevrouw?"

"Mischien wel, meneer," Theodora answered kindly. "I am seeking the imam."

"I am the imam, Madam. How may I help you?"

"Please rest assured that I am not going to cause you any trouble," Theodora said. "I was just curious. I have never seen a mosque from the inside before."

The imam looked calmly at her.

"Forgive me my ignorance, I hope I am not doing anything wrong?" she asked.

"Mosques are open to those who come in peace."

"Thank you."

"Women are actually supposed to worship from the balcony up there," the imam pointed. "So as not to distract the men while they are praying."

"Oh, I see."

Seeing that the imam was now more at ease, Theodora decided to state her real business.

"I don't want to deceive you any longer, Sir. I have come because I would like to talk to you about Riaan Meershoek."

The imam seemed taken by surprise as if he had expected no one to know about his connection to Riaan. He kept silent.

"I have come because I take an interest in his education," Theodora said.

The imam just nodded.

"He has told me that you are telling him about the Koran. He has also told me how badly he wants a proper education. I am looking for a way to help him achieve that."

The imam looked at her in astonishment.

"Please believe me. I do not know him very well, but I think you do. Is he a good person?"

"I prefer not to be the judge of who is good or bad. There's good and bad in every person," the imam said softly. "Riaan has a genuine curiosity about the world he lives in, including my religion. So I tell him about the peaceful message of Islam. He is very intelligent and kind. He really wants to learn… And he always treats my nephew Kalim well," he said as an afterthought.

"Do you think he has it in him to go to university?" Theodora asked.

The imam looked her straight in the eye.

"Oh yes, Madam. He is very intelligent. He has the most remarkable memory. I truly think that *Allah* has blessed him in that regard. Although, I admit that his blindness renders it very hard for him to reach his full potential in life. But I'm convinced he could make it at university – with a little assistance, of course. *Inshala*!"

"*Inshala*!" Theodora repeated, nodding her head approvingly. "I must talk to Lily about how we can help Riaan to get an education," she thought.

"Thank you," she said. "It makes me very happy to hear that."

Theodora turned to leave the mosque. Then she stopped in her tracks and turned towards the imam.

"Rest assured that this secret is safe with me. But please be careful. Not everybody would agree that a young man should be left to explore his ideas freely."

*

Simon's Town rowing club's pier was in full view of the club house where Lily and Theodora had suggested to Mary that they would meet for tea. They had insisted that Mary take a break from her arduous work at the hospital.

When Mary entered the tearoom in the club house, she noticed that her friends had not yet arrived. Then she heard giggling from under the window facing the pier so she leaned out to establish the source of this merriment. She noticed two young men sitting on a bench, in a secluded spot only visible from the club house if you happened to lean out of the window and look down. Both men were dressed in rowing suits but had their tops down, thus revealing their torsos. The guy with red hair was leaning up against the other young man with black hair who had his arm around the shoulders of the redhead. Between them they held a large book in a dark binding.

Mary pulled her head back in and turned towards Theodora and Lily who were just entering the tearoom. Shock was painted all over her face. She took a couple of steps back from the window. Letting her curiosity get the upper hand, Theodora too stuck her head out of the window. She lit up briefly in one of her dazzling smiles. She already knew a few things about that remarkable redhaired boy. Then she withdrew her head and turned towards the others with no facial expression at all.

"Did you see what I just saw?" Mary hissed.

The fact that the sight of two men sharing an intimate moment could upset her so much amused Theodora, considering how this explorer had described her times with practicing cannibals in her book on her travels in West Africa.

"Didn't you see the two…?" Mary seemed to search for the right term"…pederasts?"

Theodora briefly raised her eyebrows, which to Lily was a clear sign that her partner was ready to strike.

"What I saw, "Theodora answered gravely, "were two men sharing the word of our Lord."

"What do you mean?" Mary asked tersely.

"The redhead is a blind rower and from what I can see it's the Bible they are holding between them."

Mary looked unsure about how to respond. She turned abruptly and left the room, apologizing for herself saying she was just going to wash her hands before tea. Mary was ashamed at how her own loveless life occasionally made her behave erratically. Lily and Theodora looked after her in silence.

Then a triumphant smile played on Theodora's face. Lily was amused, too.

"So you think they are reading the Bible?" she asked mischievously.

"Of course, it's the Bible," Theodora answered with a twinkle in her eye. They both laughed.

"I'll take a peek, too," Lily said merrily. Quickly she went to the open window and discreetly stuck her head out. Then she turned to Theodora with a cunning expression on her face.

"You know, Theo, it's actually the redhead who is reading to the other guy. It's a braille book. That's why it's so large."

"You are so observant, my love," Theodora laughed. "Now let's order some cream tea."

*

"Did you say that the redheaded boy wants an education?" Mary asked putting her tea cup down.

"Yes," Theodora replied." He told me when I met him in Muizenberg. He had come to look for a book … but could not find it."

"What kind of book?"

"Well, if you must know, he had actually come to look for one of your books," Theodora said and she noticed how Mary blushed.

"Oh, that's really kind of him." Mary preferred not to be reminded of her many accomplishments which in her opinion were inferior to all those of her late father who had been the *real* African explorer.

Theodora could see that her remark about Riaan wanting a proper education seemed to have upset Mary.

"Did I say anything wrong?" she wanted to know.

"No, not at all." Mary paused. "I was just reminded of my childhood. I would have liked a proper education myself. But I was left to educate myself in my father's library. Actually, the only formal education my father granted me was German because he needed someone to translate for him."

"So, no French?"

"No, no French. And God only knows how useful that would have been with all the French and Belgians I have encountered in West Africa. Try and speak German to a Frenchman and see what effect that will have!" They all laughed.

"I haven't been taught any French either," Lily said lightly. "I'm not as gifted as Theodora who has a real flair for languages. She even speaks a little Xhosa."

"I grew up in the countryside, Lily, and sometimes I played with the children of the maid and servants," Theodora said modestly.

"I was free to read anything I wanted in my father's library," Mary said.

"And did you?" Lily asked.

"I most certainly did. I even managed to read enough about plumbing to keep our own system going!"

Theodora was truly impressed.

"So I can fully share this young man's wish for an education," Mary continued.

"Lily and I do too," Theodora said. "But being blind makes it so hard … His father somehow does not seem convinced about the need for him to be educated."

"There's also the cost," Lily added quietly. "Dr Meershoek already has two sons at Stellenbosch."

"The futility of education?" Mary said stunned.

"Yes. It's surprising, isn't it?" Theodora said, remembering her own limited schooling because she had been born a woman. Then she noticed a determined look on Mary's face.

"I would like to think," Mary said, "that women like us know everything about transcending obstacles? I must see what I can do!"

Theodora and Lily smiled. They both liked this young woman more and more.

"Quite so! Just because the boy is blind, doesn't mean that a useful station in life cannot be found for him," Theodora said. "There must be something we can do?"

When Theodora caught Lily's eye she could see that they were thinking along the same lines.

*

Peter was sitting on the bench outside the club house when Riaan took out a big black book from the shoulder bag he had brought to training that morning. They were both wearing their rowing suits but had the tops down.

"So this is one of the few braille books I have got, Peter."

Because he held the big book with both hands he could not orientate himself properly, so he sat down so close to Peter that their bodies were up against one another and Peter had to slip his left arm around Riaan's back.

Peter looked at the pages in the book which Riaan now opened. "It looks like a Bible," he thought. Dots were imprinted on the pages. This was the first time Peter had seen a braille book.

"These dots are just like letters in a normal book, Peter." Riaan let his fingers move slowly along a row of dots. He seemed lost in the words he was sensing.

Peter let his eyes stray over Riaan's naked torso and shoulder. His milky white skin showed where the straps of his rowing suit had been. Peter noticed that Riaan's freckles were deeper in colour where his skin had tanned.

He felt his heart beat harder. He tried to calm himself by sitting still and breathing slowly. But he felt his penis stirring under the thick book.

"So what kind of book is it?" he asked, trying to take his mind off Riaan's body. Riaan's pleasant smell and warmth made him feel dizzy and his mouth was dry. His penis was now completely erect.

"It's the Bible," Riaan said. "A priest gave it to me. I would rather have had a history book," he chuckled.

"But I suppose it's better than nothing when Kalim is not around."

The mention of the Bible made Peter shift uncomfortably.

"Are you alright, Peter?" Riaan asked.

"I just need to pee real badly," Peter said. He got up abruptly and ran to the club house hoping no one would see him.

"I am sinful," he thought. "Having an erection under the Bible!"

In the locker room he quickly stripped down and got under a cold shower.

*

In their white blouses and dark skirts, the three women strolled along the beach in their inadequate footwear in a fashion as ungainly as the few penguins they encountered among the boulders. Mary was carrying a sturdy umbrella. As she always did.

"Where do these penguins come from?" Mary asked. Animals did not usually stir many emotions in her. Except for once when she had caught a fish which she was convinced was an unknown species and which had later been named after her. But here she was taken by these endearing creatures. "I thought that penguins lived only on the South Pole," she muttered.

"There's a colony on Seal Island," Lily said and indicated somewhere on the horizon. "But we can't quite see it from here down on the beach." Lily remembered seeing Seal Island on a clear day when she had been walking in the mountains behind Simon's town.

"Do you know of a way to get to Seal Island?" Mary inquired.

Lily shrugged her shoulders. "No idea," she said.

"Maybe the rowing club could take us?" Theodora suggested. "Their heavy wooden boats can take a couple of passengers."

"May I ask," Mary said, changing the subject. "How the two of you became acquainted?"

A shadow passed over Theodora's face and she looked at Lily who suddenly seemed ill at ease too.

"Did I say something wrong?" Mary asked.

"No, not really," Lily said. "It's just that your question evokes some pain. You see, when I turned 21 and could access the considerable fortune which was left to me by my parents, Theodora, myself and a couple of other girls tried to set up a sort of women's corporative or community in Stellenbosch to be independent. I had read about how some women, during the Middle Ages in the Low Countries, had done the same and I loved the idea of living independently in a community of respectable hard-working women."

Mary stopped in her tracks. "What an excellent idea!" she decided.

"Well," Lily said hesitantly. "We thought so too, but nobody else did in Stellenbosch. They treated us more like the village witches, and after a while we had to give up. Theodora was forced to marry and had a daughter, Mariette. The other girls married too. I was the only one who chose not to marry. My inheritance allowed me not to. And I could not get myself to conform in every way."

"I know exactly what you mean," Mary said, remembering how she had nursed her sick mother while her father and brother were absent over long periods.

*

The next day, while Cousin Robert was having breakfast with Lily and Theodora in the small dining room in Admiralty House, he was busy looking through his mail.

Suddenly, he looked up and said: "Oh, here's a letter from the judge in Stellenbosch!"

Theodora and Lily looked at him in surprise. They had no idea that he had dealings with Mariette's husband. Smiling thinly, Theodora met Cousin Robert's eye. She was anxious to know the contents of the letter, but did not want to appear too eager.

"He writes that they won't be able to join us for the dinner on the Queen's birthday. What a pity, I thought it could have been an opportunity for you to see your daughter, Theodora," he said, clearly oblivious of the strife between her and her daughter because of her moving in with Lily. In fact, Mariette had not said a kind word to her mother in years.

"Thank you. How very thoughtful of you, Robert, to invite them for my sake," Theodora said lightly trying to brush her pain away.

"We went for a walk on Boulders Beach yesterday," Lily said, changing the subject. "Together with Miss Kingsley."

"Oh yes?" Cousin Robert said. "And did you come across any penguins?"

"We did, indeed. Just a few. In fact, I told Miss Kingsley about Seal Island, which she would love to visit. I was thinking that I would ask the rowing club if they might be able to take us there."

"I have a much better idea," Cousin Robert said brightly. "May I impose on you the hospitality of Her Majesty's Royal Navy?"

Lily glanced at Theodora. Cousin Robert was not normally this forthcoming. She suspected that the annual invitations to the Queen's Birthday had more to do with formality than with love for distant family members. Nevertheless, she did admire Cousin Robert for working so hard at giving everything an appearance of 'business as usual', despite all the war-related activities at the Naval Station.

"We would be most obliged, Cousin Robert," Theodora butted in with irony in her voice. "But surely you don't intend to send us three ladies to Seal Island by battleship?"

"Of course not!" he said with a laugh. "No, it won't be by battleship. I have a more appropriate craft in mind. Would you like to leave this morning, or have you got other plans?"

"As far as we are concerned, we would be happy to go today," Lily said delighted. "But I cannot answer for Miss Kingsley. I am sure she's hard at work at the Palace Barracks hospital."

"Splendid! This morning it shall be then! And not to worry, I'll send a note to Dr Carré, ordering him to 'release' his most hardworking volunteer from duty for the rest of the day. A most extraordinary woman, I hear."

And so it happened that Mary Kingsley arrived unprepared at Admiralty House. As usual, she wore a white blouse, a black shawl and a dark grey long woollen skirt. Her hair was pinned back and covered by a black bonnet tied neatly under her chin with a bow. She had brought an umbrella, although the skies did not suggest that it was going to rain. Come to think of it, Theodora had noticed that Mary always carried this sturdy umbrella around town.

Lily and Theodora were wearing light summer dresses with long sleeves to protect them from the sun and brimmed hats fixed firmly by hatpins.

Mary had greeted everyone politely, her manners being impeccable, and she seemed genuinely excited at the prospect of visiting Seal Island. Although she did ask that the excursion not take all day because she had so much work to do. Theodora could not help noticing that Mary looked extremely tired despite her best efforts to conceal it. She thought about her daughter for a moment. Mariette was roughly Mary's age, so mid-thirties, but she looked younger and less worn, given her privileged and sheltered life in Stellenbosch. Theodora again felt drawn to Mary's courage and hard-working nature, seeing in her so many qualities she would have wanted for her own daughter. Instead, she had a daughter who ruthlessly pursued her own wishes and was overly concerned with appearing 'respectable', as she loved to say.

Cousin Robert took them outside to the Dolphin Fountain from where they saw the pier at the bottom of the gardens.

"There she is, your boat!" he said and pointed. "The admiralty's launch!"

The admiralty's launch was a beautiful slim wooden craft painted in a shining dark blue and flying the White Ensign of the Royal Navy. It had a crew of seven: six sailors to row and one to steer. They stood waiting on the pier, holding their blades vertically into the air as if presenting arms. In the stern and aft the launch had a couple of cushioned seats for passengers.

"And don't worry that you are taking these sailors away from their official duties. They need to exercise if they are going to do us honour in the Championships on Her Majesty's birthday," Cousin Robert added as an afterthought before turning back to the house, leaving the ladies to fend for themselves.

And so the three women set out for Seal Island in the admiralty's launch.

Theodora studied the battleships at anchor in the harbour of Simon's town. They towered over the launch. She had never seen so many vessels here before. The place was literally packed. The British war machine was in full swing against the small Boer republics up north. The launch had to zigzag among the vessels towards the open sea.

"Do these all belong to the navy?" she asked. One of the rowers closest to her looked up.

"No, Ma'am. Not all of them. For instance that old thing over there is chartered to take prisoners to St. Helena." He pointed with his chin.

That St. Helena was mentioned anew made Theodora's heart sink. At home in Straateind, she would privately have joked that if they could produce wines in Constantia that were good enough for Napoleon in his exile in St. Helena, the same wines were certainly good enough for her. She was sure she would never crack that joke again. She kept her thoughts to herself, seeing how happy Lily appeared talking to Mary Kingsley.

As the admiralty launch passed the navy ships at anchor, soldiers took up position on deck saluting while looking with wonder at the three women being rowed in state out of the harbour.

Soon they were on open water. It was a bit choppy out here but the launch cut effortlessly through the waves. They reached Seal Island in just under an hour.

Seal Island rose only a few feet above the surface of the sea: it was more like a gigantic long rock.

"Any idea how long this island is?" Theodora asked the same sailor.

"Some half a mile, Ma'am."

"Where are you from in England?"

"From West Yorkshire, Ma'am."

Theodora nodded. "That explains his accent," she thought.

Lily pointed excitedly at the island's hundreds of Cape Fur seals and the many African penguins basking in the sun. Mary and Lily seemed really excited at the sight of so many animals. Theodora was a little put off by the stench of the guano which the wind carried right to the launch.

Suddenly Theodora jerked back from the side of the launch. She just thought that she had seen a huge dark shadow in the water disappearing under the boat. The sailor steering the launch had seen it too.

"Ease the oars!" he shouted, and the launch came almost to a standstill.

He bent down and opened a bag at his feet. He extracted a bottle with a liquid which looked like blood.

"Ladies, with the compliments of the Royal Navy, may we present you the ocean's finest predator?!"

He emptied the bottle into the water and waited for a moment. Then he got a dead chicken from the bag, which was attached to a line, and threw it into the red pool on the surface. Lily and Mary looked excitedly at the floating chicken.

At first nothing happened. Then suddenly a Great White Shark propelled itself out of the water, grabbing the chicken violently and sending a cascade of water towards the launch as it dived back in. Lily froze at the brief sight of the huge shark. Theodora was scared too, even if she had been better prepared for the sheer size of it, having seen the dark shadow in the water moments before. Mary looked on quite unperturbed.

Then another shark stuck its head out of the water next to Lily and Mary. Lily screamed at the sight of the open mouth and hundreds of sharp teeth. Mary reacted immediately and whacked the shark on its nose with her umbrella. The shark was gone as suddenly as it had appeared. There was total silence among the people on board.

"I knew it!" Mary said in her light Cockney accent. "An umbrella is just as effective against a shark as against a crocodile!"

The sailors were totally still and in disbelief over this young woman's valour in the face of such an immediate danger. Then one of the sailors said: "Bravo Miss Kingsley! Well done!"

And they all started to clap their hands.

*

Riaan sat in the kitchen. He sat immobile and listened intently, as it was his custom, while Kalim read from the *Cape Town Gazette* which Riaan's father had sent to him by train every day.

Kalim's deep and well-articulated voice had caught Riaan's attention when he had first heard it a couple of years earlier. At that time, Kalim had just taken up employment as a kitchen boy with the Meershoek household. Riaan had come into the kitchen and asked if he could have a glass of milk. Their cook, Mrs. Viljoen, had ordered Kalim to fetch Riaan a glass of milk. Their first encounter had been simple and swift. Riaan had felt Kalim's hands guide his own hands to the glass of milk and he had heard the words *asseblief baas.*

Riaan would often come to the kitchen to ask for a glass of milk or something else to drink. One day, Riaan asked Kalim if he could read to him from the newspaper that he had heard Mrs. Viljoen fold up and put down on a table. Kalim had instantly gone to pick up the paper and had started to read to Riaan.

Soon Kalim's reading the paper became part of the daily routine, and gradually he became Riaan's 'reader' instead of a kitchen boy. Dr Meershoek was well pleased with the arrangement. The two boys got on well, and with Kalim's help Riaan could move around freely outside the house. It was Kalim who first described the rowers on the bay to Riaan, whose curiosity had driven them to explore further. Before Riaan knew it, the local rowing coach had put him in a boat with a couple of other rowers. This had delighted Riaan who immediately, upon his return to the house, had asked his father´s permission to go rowing again.

Today was no different. Kalim was reading from the newspaper, although recently this took place at lunchtime to allow Riaan to practise his rowing in the morning in preparation for the Championships on the Queen's birthday.

However, this morning´s headlines on 18 May 1900 were different:

RELIEF OF MAFEKING! GLORIOUS VICTORY!

"I wonder if this is *really* good news, or just celebrating *a piece* of good news?" Riaan said aloud to himself.

They could hear commotion in the street outside. The entire naval station seemed to stir in celebration of the news. Music was heard from the nearby square where a band had taken up position, giving an improvised concert.

At that point someone knocked on the kitchen window and the face of a young man appeared.

"Who´s that?" Riaan asked.

"It's Mr. Peter, *baas*," Kalim said.

"Riaan!" Peter yelled. "Are you in there?"

Kalim quickly went to open the window, so Peter could lean in through it and talk to Riaan.

"What are you doing?" Peter said. "Come out and join the fun!"

"We're just reading the paper, Peter."

"*Arg*, can't that wait?! Just tell your *kaffir* to read it later!" Peter said aggressively.

Kalim said nothing, but took a step backwards, stunned and looking down.

"It's much more fun to be in the street now," Peter insisted.

Riaan slowly got up to face Peter. He had turned red with anger.

"Don't talk about Kalim like that! He has done you no wrong," he said. He heard his own voice tremble.

"Come on, Riaan! He's just a servant, for God's sake," Peter retorted. He felt uneasy. He had never seen Riaan look this upset before. He could not understand why Riaan was in any way concerned about a servant's feelings. That would never happen in his home. His father made sure that servants were kept strictly in their place. But he did not want to seek strife with Riaan, either.

"The eyes are useless when the mind is blind," Riaan said tersely realising now the true meaning of Theodora's words.

"What kind of nonsense is that?" Peter said impatiently. "Are you coming or not?"

"I think I'd rather stay," Riaan said.

"As you please! See you for rowing in the morning!" Peter said. He was gone in a flash. As he was running towards the square he felt stomach pain. "Why can't

Riaan just behave normally towards servants? Why do I even care about him?" He stopped briefly in his tracks at his last thought. Then he started running again, harder than before.

*

Theodora was getting dressed for the dinner Cousin Robert was hosting in honour of her Majesty the Queen´s birthday when she heard some noise coming from a group of people walking in the street past the Admiralty House. Taking a look, Theodora saw an unusual sight. Several rowing boats were being carried past the house. She had the impression that half of the village was out there, all walking towards the station just up the road.

Because of the distance to Table Bay where the Championships were to take place the following day, 24 May, all the rowing boats, including the navy's, would be taken to Cape Town by train and made ready. Only the participants from Simon's Town had this logistical problem, all other clubs being situated around Table Bay in Cape Town.

"So tomorrow's Riaan's and Peter's big day," Theodora thought. She sincerely hoped that they would do well. She had no doubt it would boost Riaan's self-esteem if they did, but more importantly Riaan's successful participation could well improve Dr Meershoek's esteem of his youngest son. She had the impression that he saw Riaan as a burden without particular prospects in life. He did not say so explicitly, she had noticed, but he always spoke with so much obvious pride of both his other sons whom he managed to send to university in Stellenbosch. Theodora did not have a shadow of a doubt that Riaan had great potential if given a chance. She was resolved to see what could be done to bring the right circumstances about.

Someone knocked on her door, so she turned away from the window. Lily came in. Theodora lit up in one of her dazzling smiles at seeing Lily who was wearing a dark blue evening dress. She herself was wearing a light grey dress.

"You look fantastic in that dress, my love," she exclaimed and came forward to take a closer look.

Lily was very good with her hands so she had made her own dress. It was the first time Theodora had been allowed to see it. Lily had been slaving away on it in her workshop behind their house in Straateind ever since they had accepted Cousin Robert's invitation. In fact, she had banned Theodora from entering her workshop, claiming that she was working on a surprise. Theodora let her eyes glide down the elegant dress and she noticed that the sleeves had a motive of dolphins embroidered in golden thread.

"These dolphins are stunning, Lily. Did you really embroider these too?"

"I would be lying if I took credit for the dolphins on the sleeves," Lily said. "In fact, they were embroidered by a Malagasy woman in Cape Town of whom I heard some time ago."

Theodora nodded her head in approval. Malagasy women were famous for their embroidery skills. Then something dawned on her and she grinned.

"Ah, so that's what Giles was so secretive about!" she said. "Not long ago I had the distinct feeling that he questioned me to find out when I was *not* going to be home."

"I am sure he did," Lily chuckled and she leaned forward to kiss her lover's cheek. "We couldn't have you wonder what was in the parcel he delivered to me, could we?"

"Are you ready, Theo?"

"Yes, my dear. I only need to put on my long gloves."

When Theodora had put on her gloves, Lily offered her arm.

"Come Theo, walk me down the staircase to the main dining room."

"Of course, my love," Theodora said, opening the door out to the upper hall. "I wonder what the dinner arrangements are?"

"I peeked into the dining room earlier this afternoon and they were doing a beautiful job of dressing up the enormous mahogany table for twenty two guests."

"Sounds like a full house," Theodora said with irony.

"Her Majesty's birthday is a serious thing, Theo," Lily said. "That's why I'm in royal blue," she laughed.

"I wonder if those sea turtles which Cousin Robert had tied up to the pier are on the menu?" Theodora said.

"Really, Theo!"

"Well, if not, I will be releasing them in the morning!"

The large mirror in the upper hall reflected the two beautifully dressed women as they slowly descended the stairs. Once at the bottom of the stairs, they made their way to the front reception room where the guests were gathering.

*

Theodora sat heavily down in front of her dresser. In the mirror she saw the face of an old woman with a tense expression around her mouth. Her ears were still ringing with the voices of the British officials at dinner, officials who were uncompromising in their belief that Britain was not only justified, but honour bound to fight for the interests of its citizens in the Boer republics. She never had nor would ever believe in any such thing as a just war! She had said nothing, mostly for the sake of not wanting to cause Lily any embarrassment. "This trip to Simon's Town was to give Lily a break away from the daily isolation in Straateind," she told herself. She had wisely retreated into the polite silence the naval officers would expect of women, while she had beaten herself up for not speaking her mind. A few times she had met Lily's gaze. She could see that Lily was aware of her lover's discomfort.

Several of the naval officers had just recently set foot in the Cape, so they had their first encounter with Africa. "They were, as newcomers, in no position to appreciate the delicate coexistence of the many communities in the Cape," she thought bitterly.

In an attempt to reassure the sensitive women at the dinner table, these men had insisted again and again that the war was going to be swift. "The war will be over before Spring," they had boasted, toasting Her Majesty again and again. Theodora had seen it as a pretext to drink as much of the French champagne as possible. They saw the relief of the little town of Mafeking a few days before as proof that the fortunes of the war had now turned decisively in the favour of the British. After the 217 day siege of the British troops under the command of Colonel Baden-Powell, they were ecstatic in their rejoicing. "It's only a matter of days before the Orange Free State will be a British Colony," they insisted. Theodora knew her kinsmen up north well. They felt an emotional bond to the red soils of Africa which would drive them to fight with extreme determination. While she did not agree with their harsh views on the natives nor their religious zeal, she did know this: like all Boers they had only one place on Earth they could call home and that was Southern Africa. For them there was no mother country overseas to idealize and turn to.

"Theo?" Lily said as she laid a hand on her shoulder. Theodora got a fright. "My dear, I didn't want to scare you, but you looked as if you had seen a ghost in that mirror," Lily said.

"More like a bad omen," Theodora whispered to herself, and she had to shake off the images of fighting and suffering in her mind. Theodora took a deep breath and straightened up, meeting Lily's glance in the mirror.

"Yes, maybe I did see a ghost in the mirror," she admitted. "A ghost of suffering to come!" She sensed that Lily shuddered. "I fear this war will last much longer than any of these military men think … and this governor, Alfred Milner, is giving me the creeps, Lily." Lily looked at Theodora waiting for her to finish her train of thought. Now, Theodora herself felt a chill at remembering Milner's cold and calculating eyes which reminded her of a giant adder waiting immobile for the right time to strike.

"Behind his impeccable manners I sense such evil, Lily." To Theodora's mind the recently discovered riches of the Boer republics could only mean one thing: the British had deliberately looked for a pretext to strike, and Milner had been the mastermind.

"I have been thinking, Theo, about our being here," Lily started softly.

"Yes, my dear?"

"When we moved to Straateind, we did so to pursue a life that would be more truly what we want. I love being here on the coast, but I also know we cannot stay forever. Nor should we. Our home is in Straateind!"

"Do you want to go home?"

"Yes, soon. Nobody is going to drive me from my home. Least of all some bigoted neighbours. We were forced to give up our Stellenbosch project. But no one will be allowed to do something like that again," she said determinedly holding her head high.

*

The cheering of the thousands of people on shore was deafening. The Table Bay Championships drew major crowds from Cape Town and beyond. This was helped by the fact that the Queen's Birthday had been declared a public holiday in the Cape.

That morning Peter had been relieved to see that on this late day in May, the weather conditions were clement.

Now the race was on!

Riaan felt overwhelmed by the shouting around him. He pushed on his footrest as hard as he could and, reversely, leaned forward all he could to create as long strokes as possible. He was scared they might fall over. He had practised for months with Peter, but he had never felt they had gone this fast. The boat was still in balance, but he knew from experience that the sculling boat would be unforgivingly unstable were they to lose their balance and coordination at this speed. His lungs felt as if they were about to explode and he had a slight taste of blood in his mouth. He sensed the water give way for their craft which they were propelling relentlessly. The two miles seemed endless. He felt the splashing of cold sea water when the oars were hammered in and out of the water around them.

"Long strokes, faster" Peter shouted behind him. Peter was sure that they had a chance to win this race over the boat from Alfred's. Britannia's had capsized a while back and the two rowers were in the process of being helped out of the water by one of the many small boats which were on the bay full of spectators.

"Long stokes! Keep the rhythm! Don't slow down!"

Riaan's limbs were starting to go heavy on him, but he kept pushing all he could as if his life depended on it. His relief was immense when he heard the horn being blown, indicating that one of the boats had crossed the goal line.

He heard exaltation in the competing sculling boat close by so he realised that they had not won. He stopped rowing and forced Peter to do the same. While his heart sank over not having won - which he knew meant everything to Peter - he felt like collapsing.

Peter and Riaan were panting heavily after their ordeal, but they said nothing. Riaan felt as if they were in a silent bubble of disappointment surrounded by the cheering from all the supporters of Alfred's team.

"Christ! Half a length!" Peter swore. "Half a length is what we lost by" he blurted out as he spat in the water.

Riaan just nodded. He knew he could not have done any better, but he also realised that Peter's military father had not brought up his son to come second.

Hands and arms lifted Riaan out of the scull as they reached the pier. Riaan felt as if he were floating in a sea of happy people. He had no sense of where he was, so he cried out: "Peter! Kalim!" His own voice was drowned out by the enthusiastic crowd. He heard female voices and sensed girls kissing his cheeks before it was as if he were flying as some strong men lifted him up on their shoulders and carried him up the pier towards land. He held on to their necks and shoulders and grinned broadly. Kalim tried to follow as best he could, being squeezed from all sides, while keeping his eye on his *baas* ahead of him. Dr Meershoek had always been very strict about him not letting Riaan out of his sight. Kalim dreaded being punished should anything happen to Riaan.

Theodora and Lily stood at the end of the pier and saw how the crowd carried Riaan off. Peter remained in his seat holding on to the pier with one hand. He watched as the girls eagerly kissed the beautiful Riaan. He felt stunned by his own heartache over Riaan and his disappointment over losing out to Alfred's. He decided that he had to stop seeing Riaan. His presence provoked such unnatural feelings in him! He had to get away from Simon's Town!

Theodora noticed that Peter had to be more than just exhausted. She quickly walked up to the sculling boat.

Peter seemed in a daze. Theodora leaned forward and stretched a hand out towards him.

"Very well done!" she said warmly. "Very well done! Congratulations!"

Only at this point did Peter notice her. He absent-mindedly grabbed her outstretched hand and felt her firm squeeze.

"Yes, congratulations," he then heard another, softer voice. He looked up and saw two slim elderly ladies. He recognised them from the rowing club in Simon's Town the previous week. He had heard that they were visitors of the admiral.

"We are so proud of you both!" Theodora continued.

"Thank you," he said meekly.

"You are not disappointed, are you?" Lily asked.

He looked at her and nodded ever so slightly, fighting back his tears.

"Participating is more important than winning – and you can take great pride in what you and Riaan have achieved today!" Theodora said. She noticed a brief shadow on Peter's face at the mention of Riaan's name. Theodora had a distinct feeling that something else was amiss with Peter, other than simply coming second in the race.

*

Riaan had bid farewell to his mother at the station. She was going to visit an aunt of his in Cape Town for the day. Suddenly Mary Kingsley appeared from the shadows under a tree, dressed in black from top to toe and carrying her sturdy umbrella. She blocked the pavement as she came walking towards them with determination. For an instant, Kalim was frightened as he saw her intense grip around the umbrella as if she were preparing to hit someone with it. So he stopped.

"What's wrong?" Riaan whispered, sensing that Kalim was tensing up.

"I am not sure, *baas*. It's the English lady from the hospital coming towards us."

And then a good-humoured "Good morning!" rang out in an accent which neither Kalim nor Riaan had ever heard before.

"Good morning, Miss." Riaan's English had a harder edge typical of an Afrikaner.

"I meant to call on you earlier to congratulate you on the good results at the Championships the other day… but I have been too busy, I am afraid."

Kalim believed her. He saw that her skin looked tired and worn despite her relatively young age. Fatigue made her look like a much older woman.

"That's quite alright … Miss?" Riaan answered lightly.

"Kingsley… Mary Kingsley."

"Very pleased to meet you, Miss Kingsley. My name is Riaan Meershoek." He reached out his hand and they briefly shook hands.

"So did you see us at the Championships, Miss Kingsley?"

"No, I'm afraid I didn't. As I said I'm very busy at the hospital. There's so much to do with all those sick Boer boys."

Kalim wondered why the English lady seemed to scrutinize his *baas,* tilting her head a little while letting her eyes wander slowly up and down his body as you would if you were buying a donkey, he thought.

"May I say how much we all appreciate what you do for us Afrikaners, Miss Kingsley? My dad speaks highly of you."

"Please don't mention it. I only do what I feel is just and must be done."

She blushed a little.

"But no, Miss Kingsley. It is no little deed! If only I could find a way of being of help, I swear to God, I would." He took a deep breath to control his sudden excitement, but in doing so he made a sobbing sound.

Kalim had rarely seen his *baas* like this. Riaan was always level-headed and stoic about his being blind, a reason why Kalim cared so deeply for him; in fact, maybe that was why everyone who met him seemed to care for him.

Mary Kingsley's face suddenly lit up in a smile and she straightened up.

"In my mind, there's not a shadow of a doubt that you will find a way to be useful. I promise you that."

Then she had turned around and walked away the way she had come.

"That was an unusual encounter," Riaan said, thinking half aloud, half to himself. He had the habit of sharing his thoughts like that when he was alone with Kalim, who knew that he probably did not want an answer. So he carried on leading him towards his home, nodding his head slightly.

A Week Later

Lily and Theodora were having tea in the loggia room when a servant showed in Dr Meershoek.

"Miss Lily! Miss Theodora! I am so sorry to come unannounced like this," he said.

He was clearly upset about something. He looked as if he had run all the way to the Admiralty with sweat coming down his forehead and his hair all awry.

Lily and Theodora got up from their tea to greet him.

"Please sit down, Doctor," Lily said. "Would you care to join us for tea?"

"Or something stronger?" Theodora asked. An eerie premonition of death had descended upon her seeing Dr Meershoek so upset. In these times of war, news was mostly very bad.

"No, thank you, Miss Lily. But I wouldn't mind sitting down for a minute," Dr Meershoek replied panting. Lily and Theodora reached for their tea cups, while looking at him intently.

"I've just had word from the hospital that Mary Kingsley has fallen seriously ill," Dr Meershoek burst out after a few moments.

"They told me that she woke up yesterday morning feeling poorly. In the afternoon, she retired to her room, and when they checked on her later in the day she was burning hot."

"What do they think has caused this?" Theodora asked.

"Dr Carré is convinced it's typhoid fever…"

"Oh no!" Lily cried out.

"And what's more, eh, unconventional," Dr Meershoek continued, "is that she refuses treatment. In fact, she has asked them to leave her be so she can die alone like an animal."

"But why?" Lily said in shock. Theodora reached out and took her hand to comfort her.

"Then all we can do is to wait and leave Mary's destiny to God," Theodora said calmly, concealing her inner turmoil.

"Dr Carré told the nurses to respect her wish. They leave the door ajar, so she can easily call them, should she want to," Dr Meershoek continued.

"They will wait in vain," Theodora thought. There was nothing she wanted more than to go and sit at Mary's bed, like the many times Mary had tended to her dying kinsmen. Still, she respected Mary too highly not to do as requested. She took a deep breath. She was sure that Mary would not survive.

"Any other news?" Theodora asked, trying to take her mind off Mary for a moment.

"In fact, yes!" Dr Meershoek said, his thoughts clearly with Mary Kingsley. "Much more trivial, of course. Peter Smith has suddenly left home. He left a note on his bed, saying that he had gone to Cape Town to enlist with the army. To fight the Boers up north."

"I see," Theodora said.

"Well, actually, he seems to have told Riaan beforehand about his plan. Riaan's very upset. He thinks that Peter's leaving somehow has something to do with him. I cannot see how his leaving could possibly have anything to do with Riaan."

"Of course, it doesn't," Lily said comfortingly while Theodora looked pensive. Lily caught Theodora's eye. Theodora sensed that Lily wanted to bring up the issue of Riaan's education which they had discussed several times since they had had tea with Mary at the rowing club.

"Dr Meershoek," Lily said sweetly. "Now that you mention Riaan…"

"Yes, Miss Lily?"

"Well, please don't be offended that I bring this up, but …"

"Please go ahead, Miss Lily."

"I know how proud you are of your boys at Stellenbosch, but what about Riaan's education?"

Dr Meershoek looked embarrassed.

"Riaan seems so intelligent," Lily continued, brushing her own discomfort aside. "So I have been thinking that I would like to facilitate his further education. You see, Doctor, I still have a small house in Stellenbosch which is locked up. But I am willing to open it up, so that Riaan and his brothers could live together while Riaan gets his education. For free, of course."

Lily and Theodora held their breath, awaiting Dr Meershoek's reaction.

"Miss Lily, that's immensely kind of you. I shall keep it in mind. Unfortunately, there's also the issue of tuition fees. Having two sons at university is already a burden. Moreover, I am not sure what sense it makes to give a blind boy an academic education."

"I see your point of view," Theodora took over, calmly but firmly. "However, I am convinced that Riaan has it in him to go to university. All he needs are braille books or someone to read to him, like Kalim does."

"Well, Doctor, should you change your view, please rest assured of my offer," Lily added.

*

At midnight Dr Carré sent word to the Admiralty that Mary Kingsley was now in a coma. Lily and Theodora immediately went on the short walk to the building next to the hospital where the nurses where accommodated.

Word had spread like a wildfire that Mary Kingsley was dying. The navy did not allow people to enter its building, so Lily and Theodora too had to wait outside in the dark. Several people had gathered there, bringing candles to keep vigil.

With the first rays of sun at dawn on that early Sunday morning, Dr Carré appeared in the door to announce that Mary Kingsley's heart had now peacefully and painfully ceased to beat.

*

Solemnly Theodora and Lily stepped up to the coffin with Mary's body. The coffin had been moved from the hospital to the main army barracks. Dr Carré took the view that Mary Kingsley was a war heroine so he had gained permission for a combined naval and military ceremony. The plate on the coffin was engraved:

Mary H. Kingsley
Aged 35
Died at Simon's Town
Whilst Nursing Boer Prisoners of War
June 3, 1900

"Thirty-five?" Theodora whispered. "I'm sure she told me that she was thirty-seven. Someone must have made a mistake. Someone should tell them."

"Let it pass, Theo, let it pass. For Mary's sake," Lily whispered back. Then they moved on to allow other people to pay their respects.

At 2 pm, the funeral party set out from the army barracks to the town jetty. First came a detachment of gunners dressed in bright blue tunics and white helmets. They were followed by the band of the Fourth West Yorkshire Regiment playing the Dead March. It was a calm and sunny but crisp winter day at the Cape.

After the military band came Mary's coffin which rested on a gun carriage. The coffin was covered by the Union Jack. The corners of the flag were held by the pallbearers, Dr Meershoek and Dr Carré being among them.

In the wake of the gun carriage came the military chaplain and a throng of mourners. Theodora and Lily walked among the nurses from the hospital who had kept watch over Mary during her last hours when she had been in a coma and could not object to their presence. Some representatives of the Boer prisoners of war had even been allowed to represent the thousands of men who were held in captivity in the prisoners' camp awaiting deportation.

Cousin Robert stood on the stairs of the Admiralty House when the cortege moved past it. All Union Jacks and White Navy Ensigns in Simon's Town were at half-mast.

Along the way, Theodora and Lily saw the faces of Simon's Town citizens who paid their last respects while watching the imposing procession moving slowly toward the sea to the solemn strains of the Dead March.

At the pier the cortege was met by a firing party of the Royal Marine Light Infantry. The pallbearers lifted the coffin off the gun carriage and carried it on board a torpedo boat.

Dr Carré, Dr Meershoek, Lily and Theodora then boarded the boat together with the chaplain and a number of marines, including a couple of military musicians.

When the boat slowly steamed out of the port, Theodora looked back. All of Simon's Town seemed to have turned out in respect. She saw that Riaan was standing with Kalim, among several other Muslims. His hair was like a dot of red in between a handful of white hats. "May God protect him!" she thought. Her inclination to help and protect Riaan reminded her of how she had always sought to help her grandson Antonius. "Where is he now?" she wondered anxiously. "In faraway Congo, I suppose. If only he would write soon. No news for such a long time!"

The torpedo boat headed due south. It had been decided that Mary Kingsley was to be buried at sea in sight of Cape Point. Around 4 pm it reached its destination. In the clear weather and calm seas, Cape Point was clearly visible from the deck. Theodora, amidst her sorrow, was awestruck by the beauty of the point which she saw now from the sea for the first time in her life. She only knew her native South Africa, but she had difficulty believing that a more beautiful Cape could be found anywhere else.

The chaplain pronounced a benediction for Mary Kingsley. Dr Carré claimed that Mary had loved the psalm *Jerusalem*, so, as the Union Jack was being removed and folded up by the pallbearers, people on board began to sing accompanied by the military musicians:

"And did those feet in ancient times
Walk upon England's mountains green:"

The coffin was carefully lowered over the deck rail into the sea and gently placed upon its surface.

"Bring me my Bow of burning gold;
Bring me my arrows of desire:
Bring me my Spear: O clouds unfold!
Bring me my Chariot of fire!"

The coffin stayed afloat on the surface. Theodora expected it would be but seconds before it would sink. After a moment, she thought that something must be wrong. The coffin kept floating slowly, drifting out at sea.

"Till we have built Jerusalem,
In England's green and pleasant Land."

The psalm came to an end. Silence reigned on board. All stared in disbelief at the coffin which refused to sink, but kept bouncing to and fro, on the waters.

Dr Carré, red faced, moved up to the commander of the marines and insisted loudly that something had to be done immediately. Quickly one of the lifeboats was readied and several of the marines, including Dr Carré, set off in pursuit of the coffin.

They soon caught up with it. After several attempts to throw out a cable to hook onto the coffin's brass fittings, they managed to haul it in. From a distance, Theodora, Lily and everyone else on board the torpedo boat squinted into the late afternoon sun at the little lifeboat and the runaway coffin.

Theodora saw that the marines had managed to attach one of the spare anchors of the torpedo boat to the coffin. They cast the anchor over the side of the life boat. It instantly sank, dragging the reluctant coffin with it into the depths of the sea, casting circles of ripples that grew wider and wider until they dissolved altogether into the smooth surface of the calm sea.

"I dare say," Theodora whispered to Lily, "that Mary had the last laugh."

*

As the northbound train departed from Cape Town, Lily sat at the window. She looked back intently towards town. Theodora got up to sit down next to Lily on the opposite bench. She followed Lily's gaze and her eyes came to rest on Table Mountain which slowly grew smaller in the distance.

Lily suddenly sighed and took Theodora's hand. "Sorry, Theo, but I cannot help it."

Theodora said nothing. She just kept caressing her lover's hand.

"You know, when you have grown up in the shadow of that mountain…"

Theodora just nodded. She knew what her English Lily wanted to say: "Table Mountain is like a magnet drawing anyone back who has come into contact with it." She certainly knew that to ring true for her partner.

"I was thinking about poor Mary," Lily continued. "Imagine coming all this way to alleviate pain and suffering…" Lily fell quiet.

"To be buried at sea," Theodora finished the sentence. "I take comfort from the fact, my love, that Mary felt she was doing something useful until the very end," she continued steadfastly.

"Theo, that day when we went to Seal Island, Mary said something strange to me."

"Yes?"

"*I have never been in love nor has anyone ever been in love with me* werc her very words. How very sad, Theo. Now she will never know how wonderful it is to love someone." Lily looked tenderly at Theodora.

"But, my dear, we know that not to be true," Theodora replied warmly.

Lily looked puzzled at Theodora who now grinned broadly.

"I am absolutely sure that half of Simon's Town was in love with her, not to mention each and every one at the hospital."

Theodora was pleased to see Lily's melancholy dissipate quickly so she decided to change the subject.

"Cousin Robert is in for a surprise which may not endear us to him," Theodora said mischievously.

"What have you done?" Lily asked, looking worried.

"Something in the spirit of Mary. Tomorrow, Cousin Robert is going to get a gift to express our gratitude for his hospitality: a cart load of bandages will be delivered to the Admiralty from Cape Town."

"Really?"

"And in our note, I encourage Cousin Robert to put the supplies to use where they are most needed," Theodora said good-humouredly.

"Oh, Theo! How lovely! I wish I could be there to see his face!" Lily laughed.

Straateind, October 1900

Theodora knocked on the door of Lily's workshop. Since they had returned, Lily had been busy working on a large canvas. Theodora had not yet been allowed to see Lily's latest painting. She was always a little coy about showing her work in progress, but this time she had been even more secretive. Theodora stuck her head around the door and saw Lily absorbed in her work. The canvas was turned away so she could only see the back of it.

Lily looked up at Theodora who quickly stretched out her right hand displaying a letter.

"This just came, my love," Theodora said. "It's addressed to you. May I come in?"

"Of course. As long as you stay at the door," Lily said with a chuckle. "Who's it from?"

"It doesn't say, but it's posted in Simon's Town."

"My hands are all dirty. Could I get you to read it to me, please?"

Theodora was eager to know the contents of the letter herself, so she quickly tore the envelope open and looked at the signature.

"It's from Riaan Meershoek," she said surprised.

"Really!? What does he have to say? Please read it to me at once," Lily said and she left her canvas to stand next to Theodora. The handwriting was a little uneven as if the letter had been written by someone not used to writing:

Dear Miss Lily and Miss Theodora,

Kalim is writing for me.

I am overjoyed that I can share some very important news with you. My father has just received a letter from London sent by the lawyer of the late Miss Kingsley. It turns out that shortly before she fell ill, Miss Kingsley had sent a letter to her lawyer informing him that should something befall her, she wanted her entire estate to go to me so that I can get a proper education.

My father has told me that you have shown an interest in my further education and has asked me to write to you, Miss Lily, to inquire whether your kind offer still stands?

Yours respectfully,
Riaan Meershoek.

PS: You may find it interesting to hear that several of the nurses at the hospital claim to have seen the late Miss Kingsley's ghost sitting next to the beds of the dying.

Lily looked in disbelief at Theodora before she jumped into Theodora's arms.

"God bless her! God bless her!" Lily shouted and she kissed Theodora on the lips, who returned her kiss.

Theodora felt like crying. She was deeply touched by Mary's foresight.

"Did she tell you she was going to do that?" Lily asked.

"No, she never mentioned it," Theodora said.

"Mary was just like you, Theo. Always capable of organising nice surprises!" They kissed again. Then Lily stood back.

"Come and take a look," Lily said and stepped towards the large canvas in her work shop.

Theodora came forward, intrigued.

What she then saw took her breath away: the unfinished canvas depicted the sea with such brilliance that it was as if the sunlight reflected back at the spectator. Every detail showed photographic precision.

Theodora laughed and hugged Lily heartily at the sight of the two rowers depicted in the sculling boat. With that red hair there was no doubt: it was Riaan and Peter at the Championships!

"My love, this is going to be the greatest painting you've ever made. Absolutely stunning! What are you going to call it?"

"I think I am going to call it 'At the Bay'".

Post Scriptum

Riaan Meershoek later became the first blind student to graduate from the University of Stellenbosch with a degree in English.

The Rhodes Foundation granted him a scholarship due to his special situation which enabled him to study at Oxford, England. He took up Oriental Studies which became his real passion.

While at Oxford, he also took up rowing again.

He later returned to his native South Africa where he sought to promote the education of handicapped people.

He never married.

He died peacefully of old age in Johannesburg, South Africa.

My Mother's Enigma

This book is dedicated to my late mother for having coached blind rowers in her youth. Rowing is but one part of the enigma which, to me, is connected with my mother. The other parts are music and singing.

My mother was a single child born into a lower middle-class family in Copenhagen, Denmark, in the 1920s. She grew up in a fairly spacious apartment in *Nørrebro* close to the city centre. Today, this part of town is one of the most ethnic places in the Danish capital so it takes a little imagination to see this as a formerly 'respectable' middle class area.

I believe that my maternal grandmother and grandfather (like most parents) would have liked my mother to climb the social ladder further. However, she fell in love with a farmer's son whom she married.

My father grew up on a smallish, rather poor farm in the middle of the Baltic island of Bornholm. Later on he took his name after this small farm hence I owe my name to an obscure locality on an island, belonging geographically more to Sweden than to Denmark.

I recall from my childhood how my mother would often refer with pride to her rowing activities in the harbour of Copenhagen. Likewise, she would talk about her playing in an amateur symphony orchestra and her singing activities before she was married. Once married, she gave up all these activities.

She never suggested that we should try rowing. Neither did she encourage any musical development in her four children. If asked about it, she would always refer to my father being tone deaf or that there was no money for music lessons. It is true that my father, to my recollection, showed no signs of being musical, but I am sure he would not have minded in the least. True, we had little money, but what does it cost to sing together with your children?

Actually, once as a boy I was singing and my mother stopped me with the words: "Stop! You cannot sing!" So I stopped, convinced that I could not sing. For years, I hated to go to church or anywhere else involving song by those attending. Later in life, when I was the only of her children living at home, I avoided playing music when she was around because she did not like music in the house. So big was my surprise when, in my 50th year, I met a singing teacher by chance who discovered that there was nothing wrong with my voice. This revelation led to me discovering one of my biggest joys: singing operatic areas by Händel.

Likewise, it was by chance that I discovered that rowing was possible in Brussels. Many people visit Brussels or live her for years without realizing that a very large canal links Brussels with Antwerp and from there with the open sea! I always send my mother loving thoughts when the sun reflects of the surface off the canal when I am out rowing.

I cannot figure out why she gave up all her interests. It cannot all have been about money. As I said, what does it cost to sing with your children? Neither can I believe it all had to do with my father. I know how accommodating he was with regard to the numerous hobbies of my sister, myself and my brothers. Neither do I want to negate the large amount of work that is involved in raising four children. Her giving up all her interests is an enigma to me.

I reconcile myself with this fact, thinking that she, like so many women of her age, gave in to social pressures, concentrating on her children and her household. Millions of women do that to this very day. Still, I have a feeling that there was something else beyond that. I shall never know.

Suggestions for further reading

Thomas Pakenham: *The Boer War*

Dea Birkett: *Spinsters Abroad*

Dea Birkett: *Mary Kingsley Imperial Adventuress*

Elspeth Huxley: *Mary Kingsley*

Mary Kingsley: *Travels in West Africa*

Mary Kingsley: *West African Studies*

Boet Dommisse: *Admiralty House Simon's Town*

———————

Lightning Source UK Ltd.
Milton Keynes UK
UKOW04n0702041215

264076UK00005B/54/P